W9-ATD-389

Monsieur Albert
Rides to Glory

Monsieur Albert

Rides to Glory

Peter Smith

illustrated by

Bob Graham

ALLEN&UNWIN

SYDNEY•MELBOURNE•AUCKLAND•LONDON

Monsieur Albert Larousse is a cycling fanatic
who lives in a tiny Parisian attic,
up six flights of stairs in apartment 6A,
a ten-minute ride from the Rue de la Paix.

He picks up the paper at breakfast one day,
and reads it while drinking his café au lait.
'Grand Cycle Race – Fabulous Prize to Be Won!'
'Magnifique!' exclaims Albert, and butters a bun.

'It's from Paris,' he reads, 'down to Nice, Côte d'Azur.
A marathon pedalling feat, that's for sure!
But I'm fit for my age and I've got a good bike,
and a fabulous prize! – that's the bit that I like!'

So elderly Albert (near hairless of head)
quickly swallows his coffee and makes up his bed.
He slips on his cycle clips, makes himself neat,
and carries his bike down the stairs to the street.

In waterproof panniers Albert has stowed
clean underwear, toothbrush, supplies for the road,
small puncture patches, a map of the route,
sunscreen and hankies, some biscuits and fruit.

He gets to the start at a quarter to nine,
after buying some bread and a bottle of wine.
'Hey Albert,' a voice yells, 'you silly old goat!
You're turning this race into some sort of joke!'

It's handsome young François, surrounded by girls,
with a sneer on his lips and a shine on his curls.
But Albert ignores the crude insult he's thrown
and pretends to be busy with thoughts of his own.

He buttons his jacket to keep out the cold
as he tries to forget that he's sixty years old.
'Come, Albert,' he says to himself, 'never fret!
There's life and there's bounce in these old muscles yet!'

There's a hush in the crowd as the mayor lifts his gun,
then an ear-splitting Bang! and the race has begun,
with a flashing of goggles and pale cyclists' knees,
and a murmuring sound like the bumble of bees.

On bumpy old cobblestones ringing his bell,
past the cafes and fountains that he knows so well,
Albert weaves through the traffic – his bike starts to sway,
but he wobbles no more on the Champs Élysées.

His glasses mist up as he steps up the pace.
He waves to the crowd that stands cheering the race.
A band plays, a drum booms, a dog starts to bark
as it chases his bike past the triumphant Arc.

'You're mad, Monsieur Albert, you haven't a chance!'
cries a gendarme (that's just a policeman in France).
'Bonne chance!' shouts a fisherman down by the Seine.
'Good luck, Monsieur Albert!' (They all know his name.)

He notices François (whom everyone fears),
a whirlwind of elbows, a clicking of gears.
He's champion of France and a millionaire;
he trains on frogs' legs and vin ordinaire.

In a shower of gravel François is gone
at incredible speed down the road to Dijon.
Old Albert is trying but hasn't a chance
of catching the cycling hotshot of France.

He stops by the road for a bit of a rest,
eats the crust of his bread (it's the bit he likes best).
The riders zoom past as he remounts his bike
and sets off again in the fast-fading light.

He's saddlesore, weary and riddled with cramp,
his trusty old jacket is wrinkled and damp.
He beds down for the night where a slow river flows
but his legs keep on pedalling in uneasy doze.

Next morning he's pumping in drizzling rain,
a trouser leg caught in the bicycle chain.
There's a puncture at Vienne, wet socks at Valence
(he'd catch the train home if he had any sense!).

Up ahead lies the way to the high mountain peaks.
With a puffing and blowing, ballooning of cheeks,
he slips to low gear as the road starts to rise,
feels an ache start to spread in his knees and his thighs.

It's onward and upward through traces of snow.
He gets off and pushes, so progress is slow.
His fingers are numb and his breath billows white
as the bitter wind moans through the spokes of his bike.

From the road up ahead comes a dull, hollow Whump!
like the air being forced from a monstrous bike pump.
There's a chill blast of wind and a shuddering groan—
it's a terrible place to be stuck on your own.

He's last to the mountaintop, covered in sweat.
The valley beneath him looks peaceful, and yet...
there's a whiteness, a shape in the faraway gloom,
like a ghost barely seen in a badly lit room.

He's freewheeling closer, down skating-rink ice,
with a squeaking of brakes like the squeaking of mice.
There's a horrible feeling of dread in the air,
and he leaps from his bike when he sees what is there.

A gigantic snowball is plummeting down,
ripping up trees and vibrating the ground,
and right before Albert's incredulous eyes
it's gaining in speed and increasing in size.

And all the brave cyclists are right in its track
as it reaches the road with a slithery smack.
Ever faster it goes in a mad downward plunge,
picking up riders and bikes like a sponge.

François sees it coming, he's still in the lead,
but can he outpace it, has he the speed?
He's a metre in front in a shower of snow —
can he avoid it? The answer is NO!

It comes closer and closer (François, it's adieu),
the snowball's engulfed him, his bicycle too,
with a glitter of snow spray and crackle of icicles,
a crunching and snapping of expensive bicycles.

It's spinning and whirling them down from the snow,
to the gentle French countryside sleeping below,
past a farmhouse, a vineyard, a peaceful old town
that's set in a patchwork of fields green and brown.

And caught in the slipstream comes Albert Larousse,
who's sucked down the road with his scarf flying loose,
sees the ball hit a parapet, leapfrog a tree
and dive like a gull in the glittering sea.

'C'est la vie,' mutters Albert, 'that's the way that it goes.
The riders will swim to the shore, I suppose.
It's a terrible thing that they're out of the race.'
(But nevertheless there's a smile on his face.)

He walks down the beach as the cyclists emerge,
helps François ashore as a wave starts to surge.
'You'll win, Monsieur Albert, go and pick up your prize!
Our bikes are all under the sea!' François sighs.

The people go wild as he rides into Nice,
with an escorting bevy of mounted police.
A hug from a film star, a kiss from the mayor,
for Albert Larousse — cyclist extraordinaire!

BRAVO! Monsieur ALBERT

It's true that the best man did not win the race,
and in bicycle races that's sometimes the case.
But François is rich (young and handsome, what's more),
so good luck to old Albert, who's sixty and poor!

For Celeste, Blye and Linda PS
For Naomi and Pete BG

First published in 2012

Allen & Unwin
83 Alexander Street
Crows Nest NSW 2065
Australia
Phone: (61 2) 8425 0100
Fax: (61 2) 9906 2218
Email: info@allenandunwin.com
Web: www.allenandunwin.com

A Cataloguing-in-Publication entry is available
from the National Library of Australia
www.trove.nla.gov.au

ISBN 978 1 74237 680 6

Cover and text design by Bob Graham and Sandra Nobes
Text hand-lettered by Bob Graham
Colour reproduction by Splitting Image, Clayton, Victoria
This book was printed in October 2012 by Tien Wah Press (Pte) Limited,
89 Jalan Tampoi, Kawasan Perindustrian Tampoi, Johor Bahru, Malaysia 80350

3 5 7 9 10 8 6 4 2